RED ORCHID

MICHAEL KINGSWOOD

CONTENTS

ABOUT THIS BOOK

George looks for his press contact, to blow the whistle on ethical issues at work.

Karen looks for her girlfriend, to patch things up after a fight.

When a mistake puts them together, their evening becomes much more interesting than either of them anticipated.

Enjoy the book! After you're done, please come to Michael's website and sign up for his mailing list at michaelkingswood.com/newsletter-signup/. Guaranteed to be spam free, he uses it to announce new releases and special promotions for his fans.

RED ORCHID

George paused inside the doorway to the back patio of Gepetto's and adjusted his tie.

He had selected a light blue one with silver-white polka dots, to offset the charcoal grey of his suit. It was a good look, he knew, and he knew the tie accentuated his eyes nicely. He would not normally dress up this way, but tonight he really needed to look the part. But the damn tie was tight.

Too tight, no matter how he adjusted it.

He knew it was just his nerves getting to him, but that knowledge didn't help.

Nor did it help to remind himself that he was the good guy here, blowing the whistle on some bad stuff that was going down. Whistleblowers were celebrated, praised.

They are also crucified, said that small voice in the back of his head that he had been fighting against for weeks, the one who told him he needed to go along to get along, not risk what he had.

And maybe he was wrong, misreading things. He didn't know the full context of what was going on in his lab. Maybe...

He knew that voice was spewing bullshit. So he shoved it aside and looked around.

Gepetto's was built of brick, and the front section was two stories tall and meticulously maintained. The rear patio was a new addition, wider than the main building, with a round knee-high pool in the center, constructed from poured concrete and designed so that people could sit on the pool's lip and converse, or just watch the water spouting from the mouth of the stone trout that was breaking surface in the pool's center.

Off to the left, a white marble-topped bar dominated, with a dozen or so stools, about half of which were occupied by customers, and every sort of bottle a man could want. A slender guy with silver hair pulled back into a ponytail, in a black collared shirt with Gepetto's emblazoned on the right breast in gold, held court behind the bar.

George recognized him from somewhere, but he couldn't place where; he had never set foot in Gepetto's until tonight.

Didn't matter, he wasn't here to chat up the barkeep.

The rest of the patio was scattered with tables, ranging from settings for two to one over in the back right corner that could take eight. They were all covered in Gepetto's black and gold table cloths, with lit candles in clear glass holders in the centers, and wrought-iron chairs that looked like they would dig into a person's back and bottom.

They were mostly filled, though, and the chatter of the various conversations almost drowned out the soft music—Italian folk from the sound of it—that came from a pair of speakers on either side of the bar.

"Excuse me," came a voice from behind him, and George half-turned to see a short black-haired guy in Gepetto's staff attire with a full tray trying to get past.

"Sorry," George said and moved out of the way, stepping off the single brick stair that led from the doorway down into the patio.

The waiter swept past, and the scents of freshly-baked bread, a basil risotto—and was that veal pic-cata?—swept over George in the wake of his tray.

Between the step and the scents of some other person's dinner, it was like a switch threw in George's mind, and he snapped to focus.

He needed to get to it.

He swept his eyes around, scanning the various customers for his contact. Or rather, for the red or-chid tucked into the hair above her left ear that she was to wear tonight, so he would know her.

He had on a similar sigil, for her benefit: a lapel button from the Boston Marathon, the one and only race of that kind he had ever run, as a bandit when he was going to college at BU.

There. The far end of the bar, last stool. A woman in a red skirt, loose for the warmth of the summer evening, and white short-sleeved, collared blouse that had the top two buttons undone. Her wavy blonde hair hung loosely past her shoulders and halfway down her back, and was held back from her face by a white hairband.

A white hairband with a red flower on the left side, just above her ear.

George drew a breath and gathered himself, then, straightening his back and pushing his shoul-ders back, he walked over toward her.

Wouldn't do to appear to be anything but

friendly. Just a normal guy out on the town. Not at all someone out for a covert meeting that could get him fired. Or worse.

As he approached the woman, he put on a smile that he hoped was warm and open.

~

Stephanie was late, but Karen found she didn't mind.

They were supposed to meet up for dinner here at Gepetto's tonight, to clear the air. Karen had suggested it; hell she had almost felt like she'd begged for it. But all the same she had dreaded the meeting all day.

It wasn't every day that your best friend accuses you of trying to seduce her husband—ex-husband, Karen corrected herself, though truth be told the signatures were not yet dry on their divorce paperwork—and Karen had no idea how to react, or how to respond. She had most certainly not done that.

Never even thought of it.

But try telling Stephanie that. Their fight had been epic, all the more so since Karen couldn't understand how Stephanie would have gotten that impression and, more to the point, why she would care what her ex did, anyway.

She had made a big point about what a pussy he was, and she was so glad to be rid of him, and she was much better off. And then she goes all jealous bitch about him?

Karen lifted her glass of chardonnay to her lips and sipped, then sniffed out a snort. Stephanie probably thought Matthew would spend his life pining away after her. Instead, word was he had turned into quite the man about town.

Though how that translated into Karen trying to hook up with him, she had no idea.

"Sellers remorse," Karen murmured to herself.

She checked her watch. Half past eight, and they were supposed to meet at eight. She had given Stephanie more than enough time, and frankly Gepetto's menu was more expensive than Karen really felt like tolerating. If she wasn't going to show, there were plenty of leftovers back at her place that she could heat up, and save some money.

Karen took another look toward the doorway leading into the restaurant's main building, and did a double-take.

The guy walking over toward her section of the bar was hard to look away from. Tall, trim but not in a skinny way; he clearly worked out at least sometimes. He was clean-shaven and had sandy blond hair, and wore a well-fitted charcoal grey suit that accentuated the breadth of his shoulders nicely. The blue tie with white dots set off the tint of his eyes, making their blue all the more plain.

It registered that he was not just coming to her section of the bar—he was coming to her—at the same time as it registered that if she could tell the color of his eyes—and such beautiful baby blues!—he was already really close, and she had been staring too long, and far too obviously.

He smiled as he slid into the empty stool next to her, and a little flutter of warmth went up Karen's body.

He nodded to her. "I'm George," he said, as though he expected her to take note, and recognize him as something special.

Karen found herself nodding in return. "Karen."

"Nice to meet you, Karen."

~

The stool was cushioned, but barely, and the contour was off just enough that it felt awkward sitting down.

For whatever reason, that semi-uncomfortable sensation dominated George's entire consciousness for a second after the woman gave her name.

He heard himself saying rotely that it was nice to meet her, and cringed inside. That sounded dumb, considering.

It wasn't like he had never approached a woman at a bar before, but this wasn't a social call, it was business. Serious business. She didn't care if he liked meeting her or not; she was here for his information.

Although, truth to tell as he got a better look at her, he truly wouldn't mind knowing her more, and not just biblically. Her green eyes flashed with intellect and she had cute little dimples that came out when she smiled as she gave her name. To say nothing of nice boobs.

Eyes up, George. This is business.

He noticed her wine glass was about two-thirds empty at the same time as the the bartender arrived at his stool.

"Good to see you again, George," the guy said, and George cursed himself again for not remembering the guy. "What'll it be?"

George cast about, then gestured at Karen's glass. "What she's having."

The bartender gave her a look, and she said,

"Chardonnay," in a tone that sounded a bit intrigued. Her right eyebrow had gone up when the bartender greeted him by name..

As the man stepped away to fill the order, George cleared his throat and said, "You've been waiting for a while," hoping that was not the case.

Karen gave a little shrug, still looking at him as though not quite able to figure him out. "Little while. I was supposed to meet someone." Her eyes flicked down as though she were annoyed, and he felt a surge of chagrin.

~

The guy, George, was clearly a regular here or the bartender would not have known him. Did he make it a habit of coming up to women like this here?

If he did, he seemed at ease with it, and he even managed to suss out she had been waiting on Stephanie.

"Sorry," he said. "I got caught in traffic."

The completely deadpan way he said that confirmed it. Definite player.

Some other night she might have told him to take a hike. But tonight, considering the reason she had been coming to meet Stephanie, and to be perfectly honest with herself, considering how long it had been since a guy who was worth giving the time of day to had come calling, she rather enjoyed the attention.

And though part of her said she should have found that notion off-putting—she was not there just for his amusement—instead Karen found herself even more interested in him.

The bartender brought George his wine, and George slipped him a twenty.

After getting his change and leaving a tip that was a bit bigger than completely necessary, George took a sip from this glass, pursed his lips in appreciation. A second later, he looked around quickly at the people nearby to them, then leaned in a little bit closer. "So how do we do this," he asked in a lower, almost conspiratorial, tone of voice. "Stay here, or go someplace more private?"

Karen blinked. He was getting a bit ahead of himself. But again, strangely, that just made her more intrigued. "Don't you think you should tell me something about yourself first?" She tried to make it sound teasing, but she heard a bit of a bite in her tone even as she said it.

He didn't recoil, though. Instead he cocked his head at her, and she saw confusion on his face. "I don't..." He shook his head, some of that assurance gone. So easily? That was disappointing. "I mean, you know where I work. What else matters?"

She blinked again. "I beg your pardon? Where you work?"

He was beginning to look more confused now, and he raised his left hand to tap at his lapel pin.

Karen had noted it, but hadn't really looked at it before. Boston Marathon? She frowned, shook her head. "You work for the marathon? But this is Miami. You on vacation or something?"

Now he did recoil, looking at her like she had three heads. "You *are* with the Herald." It was a statement, but it sounded like a question all the same.

Karen shook her head. "No, I'm a school teacher."

George mouthed, "What the hell," but didn't say it. Instead, his eyes flicked to her left ear, and he blinked, chagrin showing through on his face, followed by embarrassment. "That's not..." He shook his head. "Damn, I'm sorry. I was supposed to meet someone here, and I'd know her because she had a red orchid in her hair. I saw red from over there," he gestured toward the doorway, "and never looked again."

He shook his head and put on an apologetic smile.

Karen lifted her hand to the carnation she had slipped into her hair band. It was something she had been doing for years; wearing a flower to match her clothes. She'd forgotten why she started doing it, but continued because it felt like something uniquely hers about how she did herself up.

She hadn't met many other women who did the same, and could totally understand how it had confused George.

All the same, disappointment welled up within her, and embarrassment. For him and his predicament, but also for herself. She had enjoyed his come on, and now felt the fool.

Anger threatened to flare up, but she forced it down. It wasn't his fault, and it wouldn't be fair to lay into him.

Instead, she put on a reassuring smile. "Blind date?"

He gave a quick shake of his head. "No," he said and looked away from her. The first time he had truly looked fully away, his attention really elsewhere than her, since he had sat down, and Karen hated that she felt that lack. "Business," he added, and from the resigned, almost bitter way he voiced the word she got the impression it wasn't business he liked or wanted to dwell on.

He frowned and let out a sigh, then tensed, preparing to rise. "I'm sorry I disturbed you," he said. "I'll let you get back to your night."

Karen surprised herself by reaching out to lay a hand on his shoulder, stopping him from getting up.

He stopped at her touch, looking surprised as he turned his gaze back onto her.

She found herself flushing, but forced herself to say anyway, "My girlfriend stood me up, and... Well, I can't stand the idea of eating alone tonight."

Even as she said it, Karen knew it was true, and that she had been lying to herself earlier about being perfectly happy with leftovers at home, alone. Even if she couldn't make up with Stephanie—and maybe even if she could—after the emotionally draining day she'd had, she really just needed...company.

And George's promised something...she didn't know what it was.

But she really wanted him to stay, that she was certain of.

When Karen put her hand on his shoulder, George felt a rush of heat travel from where she touched him to every square inch of his body.

Her invitation redoubled that heat, and he felt sure he was flushing. "I..." He stopped, swallowed. "Are you sure? I don't want to impose."

Her fingers tightened on his shoulder and she nodded, and suddenly he saw a deep need in her eyes that reflected his own. But while his was the need to get the word out about the chicanery going on at his company, the possibly illegal and certainly dangerous things going on in the labs there, hers was....something else, but something equally real for her.

Whatever physical attraction he had felt for her —and there was enough of that—faded in the light of the sensation of mutual distress that he felt radiated from himself to her and back.

Even if she had been a land whale, he didn't think he would have wanted to say no to her request, right then.

But he did still have business to take care of.

Nodding, he said, "I'd like that. But I do need to take care of this one thing." He saw disappointment in her eyes and hurried on before she could give it voice. "Let me make one more round through, to make sure I didn't miss her. I'll come right back."

She hesitated, then nodded.

He left his wineglass on the bar, to show he would be returning. But when he turned away he had the distinct impression she thought he was shining her on.

He moved quickly through the patio, checking all the faces at the tables and the bar—and periodically glancing over to make sure Karen hadn't decided to just go—and did not see his contact anywhere. He was about to turn back to Karen, but decided he really should check the front of the restaurant, just to be safe.

He knew tomorrow he'd want to be able to say he really had put forth every effort here.

But a look through the front building was just as fruitless as his look around the patio had been. In the bar near the entrance, with its old-school mahogany finishwork and warm but dim lighting, in the main dining room, sprawling and filled with hand-carved darkly-stained tables for parties of all sizes, topped by Gepetto's tablecloths and candles, to the three private event rooms upstairs—all locked except one that was taken by a private party, or so the maitre'd said and no he couldn't go in—there was no sign of the woman from the Herald.

She must not have taken him seriously after all.

Feeling almost insulted, George headed back down the softly-lit hallway that led from the main dining room, past a connecting hallway for the bathrooms, and to the back patio.

He should have felt relief, that he didn't actually have to go through with this thing. Instead irritation that he knew would quickly turn to anger began to kindle. What was he, chopped liver, that they wouldn't even look into what he was trying to tell them? If they -

"If you're done flirting, how about we get down to business?"

The voice, low but still feminine, came from the hallway to the bathrooms just as George was walking past it.

He stopped and turned quickly, on guard.

The woman there was short, maybe five foot even, on the heavier side, and in her mid-fifties. She wore a navy blue pants suit with a white collared blouse beneath her jacket, and eyeglasses that re-minded him of his High School librarian. Her hair was fully grey, and done up in a bun, and she wore a businesslike expression on her face. Her eyes shined with intellect, but he thought he saw a hint of amusement in them as well.

But what he lingered on most as he looked her

over was the red orchid she had tucked behind her left ear.

He felt as though a weight had lifted, and all the doubts he had been harboring slipped away. He grinned and stepped toward her.

"Let's do this."

~

Karen highly doubted George actually meant to come back, whatever he had said. But still, she found herself hoping he would.

But after he vanished into the doorway leading back into Gepetto's main building and then didn't reappear for several long minutes, she knew for certain.

He had ditched her.

Just like Stephanie had.

Stephanie's betrayal—and her accusations were a betrayal, whether Stephanie wanted to think so or not—had hurt. Hurt a lot. But somehow George's leaving tonight stung in a more profound way, going straight through to the core of her womanhood.

How could Stephanie actually think she could seduce her ex even if she had wanted to?

Karen shook herself. Enough of that kind of grousing. She waved the bartender, Sam, over and got the bill for her wine.

She did not spend any time on self-pity as she bent over and picked up her purse from where she had left it at the foot of her stool, fished out the money to pay for her drink, and paid Sam.

She definitely did not. She wouldn't feel that sort of thing over some random guy she'd just met and had only talked to for five minutes. That would be silly.

Looping her purse over her shoulder, Karen stepped off her stool and turned away from the bar.

George was right there.

The smile he had been wearing slipped as he looked from her to the money on the bar and to her purse.

"Leaving?" He clearly tried to hide it, but she could hear that he really didn't want her to.

She shook her head but stayed silent, not entirely trusting herself to speak. The rush of feelings when she saw he hadn't left after all—relief, annoyance with herself, anger at being annoyed, embarrassed about being angry, happiness, and lastly an odd hope—left her uncertain what she would actually say, and she had learned long ago that it was best to just shut up in those sort of situations.

His smile returned, and Karen only now saw that before, warm as his smile had seemed, it had not fully gone through to his eyes. But now, it seemed like some burden had been lifted from him, and she sensed peace flowing from him.

It felt good; it was a feeling she wanted.

"Hello Karen," George said, and held out his hand. "I'm George. I work in biotech."

Karen returned the smile and shook his hand. "It's nice to meet you, George."

MESSAGE FROM THE AUTHOR

Thank you for reading my book. I hope you enjoyed reading it as much as I enjoyed writing it.

Every review helps an author out, so whether you loved this book, hated it, or something in between, please take a minute to tell other readers what you thought. All of the online retailers make it very easy to do, and I would really appreciate it.

Feel free to come say hi at my website or on Facebook. I always enjoy hearing from readers, especially since you all are, collectively, my boss.

I also have a weekly podcast, Story Time With Michael Kingswood, where I read stories and talk through some of the latest goings on in my world. I'd love to see you there.

Thanks again. My best to you and yours.

Warm Regards,
Michael Kingswood

MAILING LIST

If you enjoyed this book and would like word on new releases and special deals from Michael Kingswood, sign up for his newsletter on his website. Guaranteed to be spam-free, you can opt out at any time. And you can rest assured he will not share your information with anyone, for any reason.

https://michaelkingswood.com/newsletter-signup/

SUPPORTING PATRONAGE

Michael would like to invite you to become a supporting member of his website. Similar in concept to Patreon, a few dollars a month will give you access to exclusive content, and help him to focus more of his time to writing fun and exciting stories for your enjoyment.

Sign up at his website:

https://www.michaelkingswood.com/membership/
supporting-patronage/

ABOUT THE AUTHOR

Michael Kingswood is 20-year veteran of the US Navy submarine force and a lifelong fan of science fiction and fantasy literature. His work has appeared in numerous collections and anthologies, to include the Fiction River Anthology series from WMG publishing. He holds a bachelors degree in Mechanical Engineering as well as a Master of Engineering Management and a Master of Business Administration. He has four children and currently resides in San Diego.

Find Michael Kingswood online at:

www.michaelkingswood.com

www.facebook.com/michael.kingswood

steemit.com/@michaelkingswood

MORE BOOKS BY MICHAEL KINGSWOOD

Glimmer Vale Chronicles

Glimmer Vale

Out-Dweller

Tollard's Peak

Robbed Blind

Wedding Gifts: A Glimmer Vale Chronicles Story

The Falconer's Stairs

Glimmer Vale Omnibus Edition #1

The Pericles Conspiracy

Passing In The Night

The Pericles Conspiracy

Dawn Of Enlightenment

Masters Of The Sun

Novellas

What Lurks Between

The Necromancer's Lair

The Champion

Veritas Morte

Story Collections

Tales Of Adventure #1

Tales Of Adventure #2

Short Story 10-Pack

A Jar Of Mixed Treats

Short Fiction

Michael has also published a number of shorter works,
links to which can be found on his website.